THE MOVIE STORYBOOK

Adapted by Tony Oliver

Based on the screenplay by John Kamps and Arne Olsen

Now a major motion picture from 20th Century Fox

Book Design: LITCO Marketing

Illustration: Dan Burrus

A TOR® BOOK

Published by Tom Doherty Associates, Inc.

175 Fifth Avenue, New York, N.Y. 10010

This book is printed on acid-free paper. Tor® is a registered trademark of Tom Doherty Associates, Inc.
ISBN 0-812-54454-4
Printed in the United States of America
0 9 8 7 6 5 4 3 2 1

TM

It was a glorious afternoon as the citizens of Angel Grove gathered for a city-wide fund-raiser and festival. The highlight of the day was a skydiving contest featuring skydiving teams from all around. The crowd cheered loudly as Rocky, Adam, Aisha, Billy, Kimberly and Tommy, the team from Angel Grove High, landed right on target and took first prize for the day.

Meanwhile, in another part of the city, a group of construction workers uncovered a strange object. It was shaped like an enormous hand holding a giant egg. Smoke swirled around the object as it glowed with a strange purple light. Slowly, the workers approached the eerie object. One of them tried to touch it but was thrown back by a bolt of energy. The remaining workers had seen enough and ran for cover.

Up on the moon, the discovery of the object caught Lord Zedd's attention. "I've been looking for that egg for two thousand years," he said as he waved his staff and teleported with Rita Repulsa, Goldar and a creature named Mordant to the construction site. Once there, he used his staff to send a beam of magic into the egg, causing it to split down the center and open. Inside was gooey purple slime. "You waited two thousand years for this tub of goo?" screamed Rita.

Suddenly the goo in the egg began to churn and boil. A column of goo began to rise from the egg and take the shape of a hideous purple man. The morphological being stepped out of the egg and introduced himself. "Ah! I'm Ivan Ooze and I'm back!" Lord Zedd quickly stepped up. "Ooze, I am Lord Zedd, sworn enemy of Zordon of Eltare, and –" "Zordon?" interrupted Ooze. "So he's still around, huh? Well, not for long."

Meanwhile, at the Power Rangers' Command Center, Zordon had become aware that the egg had been uncovered and called the Power Rangers to warn them of the dangers. "Six thousand years ago an evil sorcerer named Ivan Ooze was imprisoned in a hyperlock chamber under Angel Grove. The chamber has been uncovered. You must return it to the depths of the Earth before Ooze can escape." "We're on it, Zordon," replied Tommy, and the Power Rangers teleported away.

By the time the Power Rangers arrived at the construction site, Ivan Ooze had turned against Rita and Lord Zedd and trapped them in a tiny snowglobe. He seemed to know the Power Rangers were there before he even saw them. "Hmm..." he muttered, "it smells like...teenagers." "Not just any teenagers," shouted Tommy. "We're the Power Rangers!"

"So what? Am I supposed to be impressed?" sneered Ivan Ooze. With a wave of his hand, a dozen globs of ooze appeared on the ground and grew into fierce warriors. Ooze said, "Nice knowing you," and disappeared in a flash. Ooze's army then charged the Power Rangers. The battle was on! With great skill and valiant efforts, the Power Rangers fought hard against the gooey warriors, but they proved too strong and the teens had to pull back. Tommy shouted out the command, "It's Morphin time!"

In a flash, the power of the morphing grid surrounded the teens and morphed them into their Power Rangers suits. Despite this, the warriors continued to attack. It was all the Power Rangers could do to keep from being defeated. Slowly, however, the tables started to turn and the Power Rangers began to eliminate their opponents, one by one.

As the Power Rangers fought for their survival, Ivan Ooze slithered his way into the Command Center to confront his old enemy, Zordon. "Still hanging around, Zordon?" mocked Ooze. "It's time I pay you back for locking me up in that rotten egg." Zordon vowed, "You'll never get away with this, Ooze." Ooze just laughed. "I've got a news flash for you...I already have." With that, Ooze waved his wand and began to completely destroy the Command Center.

Back at the construction site, the Power Rangers continued to battle Ivan Ooze's army. They discovered that if the warriors were hit hard enough, they would break apart into globs of purple ooze. One by one, the Power Rangers kicked and slammed Ooze's men until they were all gone. But then something strange happened – the Power Rangers began to de-morph. Before they knew it, all their powers left them, and they were back in their normal clothing. "We'd better get to the Command Center and find out what's going on," said Tommy.

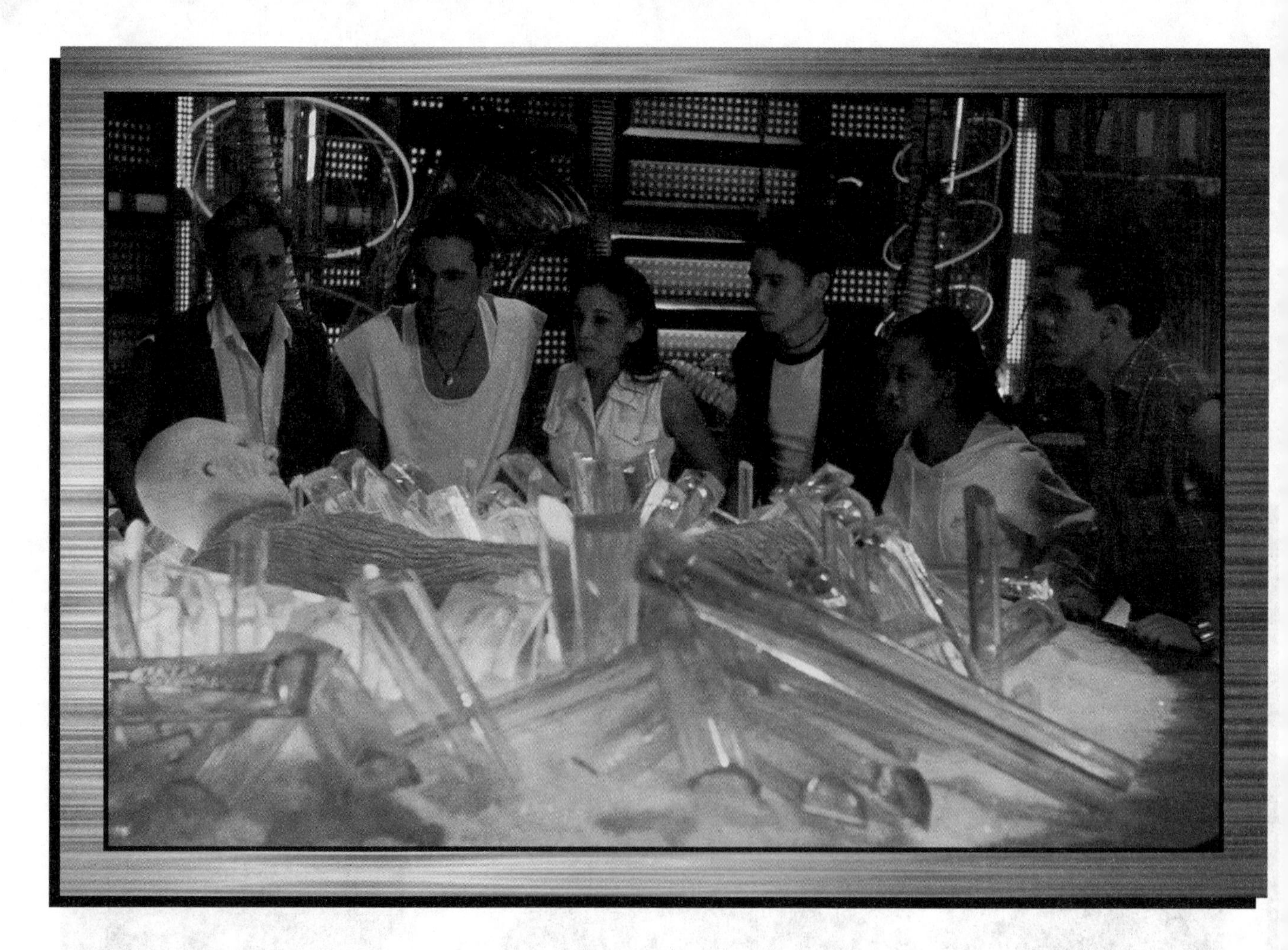

Without power from the morphing grid, the teens had to make their way to the Command Center on foot. When they finally arrived, they found the Command Center in shambles. Alpha 5 was barely functioning and Zordon was outside his time warp in a heap of twisted glass and metal. "What happened here?" asked Tommy. Billy exclaimed, "Zordon's in trouble! Outside his time warp he's aging at an accelerated rate. We've got to do something."

Zordon spoke in a whisper. "What you must do is find the Great Power of Phaedos and use it to defeat Ivan Ooze. It is your only hope." Alpha 5 explained, "It's not a who, it's a where. Phaedos is a distant planet. You must travel there and find an ancient pyramid – the source of the Great Power. Hurry, Power Rangers, Zordon doesn't have much time." "Right," said Tommy. "Let's go Power Rangers!" Alpha pushed a series of buttons and sent the teens off in a colorful rainbow of light.

Meanwhile, back in Angel Grove, Ivan Ooze continued to advance his plan to take over the world. Masquerading as a clown, he spread his gooey ooze all over town. The ooze had magical properties that turned all of the adults in town into mindless zombies, while causing the kids to go wild and misbehave. "Ah, just like old times," laughed Ooze.

The Power Rangers traveled across the cosmos and eventually landed on the beautiful but strange planet of Phaedos. There they sought out Dulcea, the Warrior Princess, who once fought against Ivan Ooze with Zordon. She empowered the teens with the secrets of the ancient Ninjetti and sent them through the jungle in search of the Temple of the Great Power.

Back on Earth, Ivan Ooze had gathered all of the mindless adults and put them to work making purple ooze and building a new robotic monster with which to terrorize the planet. The kids of Angel Grove, now fully under the magic spell of the purple ooze, were running wild through town, vandalizing their homes and shops and schools. Ooze was very pleased with himself. "It's so good to be on top again. And this time, no Zordon or Power Rangers to stop me!"

Meanwhile, the Power Rangers had traveled through thick jungles and over steep mountains to find the Temple of the Great Power. In the center of the temple was a large pyramid. In the center of the pyramid was a large glowing shield with pictures of the Ninjetti animal spirits – Bear, Wolf, Crane, Frog, Ape and Falcon. These spirits were the sources of the Great Power.

Now armed with their new powers, the Power Rangers were able to morph and teleport back to Earth to save Zordon and the world. When they arrived in Angel Grove, they could not believe their eyes. Destruction was everywhere. The streets were littered with broken glass and burning cars. "Looks serious, guys," said Tommy. "We'd better call up the Zords."

The Power Rangers raised up their hands to call on their new powers. "I call on the power of the Falcon!" shouted Tommy. "I call on the power of the Crane!" cried Kimberly. Each Power Ranger followed, calling forth the Ninjetti powers. Instantly, their new Zords appeared.

With a great leap, the Power Rangers flew up in the air and landed inside each of their Zords. They came together to form the mighty Ninja Megazord, preparing for the battle to come. "All right, Power Rangers!" Tommy shouted. "Let's kick some Ooze!"

The Zord came alive with power. All systems were up and fully charged. Streaks of lightning swirled around the huge Zord as the Great Power of the Ninjetti ran through the new vehicle's circuits. With weapons ready, the Power Rangers guided their new Megazord into the heart of the destroyed city in search of Ivan Ooze.

Suddenly, Billy remembered that soon a comet would be passing through the Earth's atmosphere. The Ninja Megazord lured Ivan Ooze into space for a final confrontation. Ooze was ready for them. He expanded his powers to gigantic proportions and attacked the Ninja Megazord, nearly defeating the Power Rangers.

Ivan Ooze and the Megazord struggled with each other as the comet came closer and closer. "Give it all we've got!" Tommy ordered. "If we don't beat him soon, we're all goners!" The Power Rangers sent a power burst through the Zord, causing Ooze to break away and tumble out of control into the path of the comet. When Ooze and the comet collided, a great explosion lit up the skies over Angel Grove.

With Ooze gone, the spell over the city and its citizens was broken. The Power Rangers used their newfound powers to restore Zordon to his time warp and to re–energize the Command Center. The citizens of Angel Grove declared a Power Rangers Day and held a huge celebration in their honor. The Power Rangers had, once again, saved the world from the forces of evil.